I DARE YOU

I DARE YOU

A NOVELLA

DOROTHY DODSON MARCY

BELLE
POINT
PRESS

Fort Smith, Arkansas

I Dare You

Edited by Casie Dodd
Design & typography by Belle Point Press

Belle Point Press, LLC
Fort Smith, Arkansas
bellepointpress.com
editor@bellepointpress.com

Find Belle Point Press
on Facebook, Substack,
and Instagram (@bellepointpress)

Printed in the United States of America

29 28 27 26 25   1 2 3 4 5

Library of Congress Control Number: 2025931856

ISBN: 978-1-960215-31-4

IDY / BPP40

1

Saying Goodbye

Judith was twelve and facing the biggest challenge of her life. It didn't seem fair. This year was supposed to be different. She wasn't supposed to be playing games with her sister all summer to fend off the boredom of long, hot nights. It was 1953, a year of tying things up and moving on, her last chance to be a child. This year she would turn thirteen. She would become a teenager, so this summer she had to finish climbing trees, playing cowboys, and hunting for arrowheads. She had to finish exploring the woods behind their house before she was forced to see Fort Smith, Arkansas, through different eyes. It was a saying-goodbye year, and she wasn't looking forward to the next one. Dragging her feet, and trying to slow time down, she wanted to make the best of her last free year. She needed to squeeze every drop of life out of each moment because she would never have the chance again.

Judith had carefully studied teenage girls. She knew what they were like. She watched them stand at the bus stop every morning before school in ponytails, their felt poodle skirts and saddle oxfords. She saw them fuss with their hair and makeup and become helpless in the presence of boys, and she didn't want any part of it. It wasn't just the colored girls in her neighborhood either. She knew that all teenage girls were this way; the white girls too became helpless and stupid when they became teenagers. She just wanted to be Jude, the one who kept her sister entertained with adventures only she could create. How could she become a "Southern Belle," wearing can-cans and bobbysocks? She would not have it, and yet she couldn't escape it. She didn't want to be a boy, but she didn't want to be a girl either.

Actually, that wasn't true. Sometimes she did want to be a boy. She had spent her twelve years watching her brothers live a life of freedom, while she and her sister were quietly being shaped into something she didn't want to be. The boys rolled out of bed each morning, downed a bowl of Corn Flakes and they were gone, out the back door, onto their bikes and out into the world, while she and Vivian had to be correct and hygienic, getting their hair combed and braided, being careful about which body parts were showing.

She did like being a girl, liked girl things—dollhouses, coloring books, paper dolls, girls' clothes that had so much variety and color—but she didn't want to be like *those* girls. She didn't want to wear fingernail polish and pumps. So she was surprised and relieved when she received the dare—a great distraction from her worries and possibly the hardest thing she had ever done.

Her mom seemed to know there was something more in the air that year too. Jude could tell that her mother was fussing over her a bit more than usual. This was the year she brought her the "training bra." *What a joke!* She heard the front door slam that afternoon when her mother breezed into the house from shopping, out of breath and flushed with excitement. Something was up; she knew it. "Judith Ann." Her mother called her in a singsong voice that drew out the *An-n-n-n* into about three syllables. "I have a surprise for you!" she sang some more, paper rattling as she riffled through packages and tissue paper.

Judith was in the back bedroom with her sister when Viv whispered, "It's a bra!" Viv was four years younger, and because she was small, she could be present around adults and they wouldn't notice her. That way she knew things way before her four siblings did. Judith's heart sank: *No more playing cowboys and being "Little Beaver" shirtless with a feather stuck in her headband.* A training bra! She had nothing to train! There were two little walnut bumps on her chest, and that was all. It was her mother's friends who had bosoms that needed "training," their uncontrollable breasts heavy and unmanageable.

Now she would be teased by the boys because they could see the outline of bra straps beneath her shirt. They would sneak up behind her, snap the straps and run away laughing. Jude answered her mother's call and put on a stoic face, standing there while her mom brought out the surprise, a contraption that consisted of two very flat triangles of cloth (no cups at all), with straps and a band that hooked together at the bottom. In that moment, life for her had changed forever, and she knew it.

There was more to come, she thought, and already she didn't like it. What would Christmas be like once she turned thirteen? No more toys? Only clothes, lipstick, and nail polish? She and most of her friends still played with dolls. Just this year her doll, Betty, had been invited to Cyrus' birthday party. Cyrus was Jo Ann's doll, and they lived in the house across the street with Jo Ann's grandparents. The invitation had come in the mail, making it a really special occasion, and Mrs. Dobbs, Jo Ann's grandmother, even baked a cake for it. The two of them had taken the bus downtown one Saturday to shop together for Cyrus' birthday presents. On the big day they sat in the little house in Jo Ann's backyard, eating cake and ice cream, their dolls on their laps, and complained about how unruly their daughters were.

The problems Jude faced were little-girl problems. She wanted to put a ribbon in Betty's hair although the hair was actually painted onto a head made of pressed sawdust. She had finally resorted to raiding her dad's toolbox, borrowed a hammer and nail, and attached a pretty pink ribbon to Betty's head. She had a vague sense that this was doll abuse, but it had to be done. She did not want to leave this world of make believe and fantasy to enter the world of prissy young ladies.

Jude could already envision her thirteenth birthday, summer ending and her mom going over the top with the celebration:

a big family party, a huge cake with candles lit, enough gifts to make her self-conscious and embarrassed, and a dramatic speech from her mother about the excitement of becoming a teen. It would be her mom's chance to redo what she had wanted at this age, but it wouldn't be what Jude wanted. She wouldn't want the attention or any of the gifts, only the one from Vivie who would probably give her something cool, like a pocketknife. That she would cherish.

Jude loved her mom and really wanted to please her. She knew she would never be the ladylike girl her mother wanted, but she tried her best. Growing up in a house full of women who were proud of their domestic skills put a pressure on her that was hard to balance with the girl inside who loved to run and climb and try new things. She would never settle for cleaning and cooking for the white families of their town, like her grandmother and aunts did, but she tried to be that girl at home, just to please her mom. She learned to do the military fold when making the beds, and ironed handkerchiefs and dresser scarves to her mother's satisfaction. She even tried to make a pound cake, and with her mother's guidance she succeeded. Mrs. Johnson was so proud that she bragged about her daughter's cooking skills to all her friends, but the next one Jude made was done without her mother looking over her shoulder and it was more like a ton cake. Mrs. Sanders, her mom's best friend, said, "Jude, you're not supposed to put in a pound of every ingredient!"

Mrs. Johnson had graduated valedictorian of her high school

class and was brilliant. Her head was full of poetry and her vo-cabulary was full of four-syllable words. Her plans for college had been derailed when the Depression hit in 1929, but she had simply channeled her brilliance and creativity in another direction. She had become the town's public speaker, and every organization, both black and white, wanted her to speak at their Mothers' Day programs, their annual ice cream socials, their Memorial Day celebrations. Jude was proud of her and wanted to make her mother proud too, but she knew she would never be the proper lady her mother had been. She would do her best, but her skills lay in another direction. She would be the best big sister she could and Viv's best friend.

2

Best Friends Forever

Judith and her sister had been best friends from the moment Vivian was born. Jude was four and Viv was her living, breathing doll. As she grew, their friendship did too, and they made mud pies together, icing their pies with flower petals. They made clothespin dolls with corn silks for hair, and played beauty shop, school, and church, imitating the adults in the house. Viv was the baby of the family for eight years before their little brother came along, and that was long enough for her to charm her way into all their hearts—even Grandmother's, who was not the kindest person under the best of circumstances. Grandmother was a staunch Baptist and thought it was sinful for children to have too much fun. Everyone else in the family was Methodists, AME, and a little more relaxed about life, but Grandmother stood her ground. Any fun, especially on Sundays, was a sin against God.

But Jude and Viv had as much fun as they could squeeze out of their day-in and day-out existence of doing the dishes, school, and homework. They never fought like most sisters, who competed with each other and complained to their parents that one was unfair or the other was mean, but it was probably circumstance that cemented their friendship.

Although they lived in a two-story house with four bedrooms, their father had an open-door policy with regard to relatives who were down-and-out, so there was never enough room. With the aunts and their daughters and the uncles who couldn't find jobs, the house was sometimes full of day beds and roll-away beds, folks sleeping on the sofa in the living room and pallets on the floor. Their quarters were cramped, and no one in the house had much time or space for solitude. The girls wore hand-me-downs from older cousins, and were a united front against the boys who wanted to use their dolls as captives in their games, hanging them from their gallows. Kids in the neighborhood thought the girls' closeness was odd and told them so. "All sisters fight," they said, but Jude and Viv just shrugged their shoulders and replied, "We don't." Jude loved their close connection.

Their parents were highly respected in the little colored neighborhood. Her mother was PTA president, head of her Stewardess Board at the AME church, and an officer in the Eastern Star. Her dad was a Mason but he was not so involved in community affairs, although he was just about the most likable guy in town. Mr. Johnson was known as a "square dealer" because of his honesty and integrity. Even the banks in town would give him loans without collateral, just on his signature. But he also had a drinking problem. Few people knew about it because he was a happy drinker who came home from work every day, a half pint of Evan Williams in his hip pocket, and spent his evenings singing and dancing for his children.

The children would sit together on the sofa and encourage their dad to dance for them. "Do the clown dance, Daddy!" they would yell in unison. And he would put a record on the turntable and start the dance, one finger on top of his head and the other hand above his hip, much higher up so that he looked intentionally ridiculous. He would turn in a circle, bending his knees in a dipping movement as he circled round and round. They loved it! Nobody else's dad was that much fun. When he wasn't dancing for them, he told them stories, sang to them, or created riddles for them to solve. Jude loved how close and self-contained they were. The town, by excluding them from much of its functioning, had made them self-sufficient.

On the morning of the day that changed her life, Jude sat in the glider in their front yard wishing for excitement, not knowing what was coming. She watched clouds drift across a clear blue sky, longing for adventure, and wished she lived somewhere more interesting. The colored neighborhood was even more boring than the rest of the town. Every adult felt responsible for parenting every child and they had their eye on her, which meant she couldn't breathe without her parents knowing about it before she got home. She still resented Miss Walton, who had called her into her house one day and given her a whuppin' for walking down the street with her hair uncombed. Miss Walton had then called her mother and reported the incident so that Judith got into more trouble when she got home.

Except for the fun of being entertained by their dad, events in their neighborhood were all routine: church on Sundays, sunrise-service on Christmas mornings, Christmas and Easter programs in which she had to recite the dreaded singsong poems. Monday was laundry day, Tuesday was ironing; even the menus for suppers were scheduled with Sunday chicken and Wednesday meatloaf. White people lived in a world where rules could change whenever a colored person's actions offended them, but in her neighborhood everything was orderly and predictable, no surprises.

Jude wanted to live in a city, the kind she saw on television. Television was their window to the world. Jude and her siblings had begged their dad to get a TV, promising never to ask to go to the movies again. Their dad had come home one day with a Raytheon, a huge mahogany frame around a very small screen of a television. The family gathered around it every evening when supper was over and dishes were done. Dad presided over the television watching, with the lights turned off except for the TV lamp, and no one was allowed to talk. They watched *Dragnet* and *The Naked City* and Jude learned about the world outside the small, cramped neighborhood the town had set aside as her world.

She wanted to live in an apartment, with a stoop. Her parents had bought their house in 1940, the year she was born, and it was all she knew. She was itching for something different. Sometimes she even wished her parents would get a divorce. Their house wasn't calm and orderly with so many people moving in and out, but she never heard her parents fight or even argue. It would be so cool to live with her dad, have a single parent and be in an apartment in the city.

Vivian, who took after her dad as the entertainer of the family, could find humor in just about everything and was a genius at getting out of doing her chores. She was thin and anemic and could feign sickness whenever it was convenient. Occasionally, on a cold morning when the bed felt especially warm and comfortable, Viv would whisper to Jude, "I'm not going to school today." She would drag herself down the stairs and into the living room wearing a tattered bathrobe, which she clenched together at her chest, although she could have easily buttoned and belted it. Her hair uncombed, she'd sit by the big living room stove and cough until an adult noticed her. She even seemed to be able to make herself look pale and thinner. Only after they had noticed her would she say, "I don't feel good." That was it—she would have to say no more to get the day off from school. It never worked for Jude, who just looked too healthy.

When there were chores to be done, Jude ended up doing them herself, but she never minded it because Viv entertained her. It was Jude's job to teach her younger sister all the domestic skills their mother had insisted she learn, like how to properly make a bed.

"The corners are to be tucked in 'hospital style,'" she'd tell Viv, but Viv's response was always "Why make it up? We're just going to get back into it tonight, anyway."

"Because Mamma said we have to. Anyway, we have to take the sheets off and put on fresh ones."

"Aw, let's leave 'em dirty. It makes it easier to slide back into bed at night." They would both laugh, and Jude would change the sheets. Sometimes Viv just made up funny ways to walk out of the blue. "Watch this," she'd say. Before long Jude would be in stitches.

Viv was Jude's saving grace. She knew she was lucky in a lot of other ways too. Although they weren't allowed to eat in restaurants or use public bathrooms and drinking fountains, their family owned their house. Most of the people she knew were renters. She got whuppins with switches from the pussy willow in their front yard, but all kids got those and she was never injured by her parents—like some of the kids at school who were hit with whatever was close at hand. Their whuppins, like everything else, were methodical and followed a prescribed pattern.

"Go get me a switch," one of the adults in the house would say. She would search for a suitable one from the willow tree in the front yard with its long, graceful branches, knowing that if she brought in a puny little one, she would get extra punishment for that. She liked to think of that tree as the "whuppin' tree."

She would get the usual speech about how this was gonna

hurt them more than it hurt her. *Well, you are the one with a choice here,* she always thought. The speech was followed by the whuppin', the adult asking over and over with each strike from the switch, "Are you gonna do it again?" and the child giving their prescribed response, "I ain't gon' do it no more!" When she and her siblings had done something their mother thought was awful, they would get the belt from her dad, which wasn't as bad as it seemed because Dad had spent the day at work and was not upset about whatever had happened.

She found herself grateful for her parents' restraint, knowing that not all parents had it, and there was no Child Protective Services, no recourse for a child who was bruised and blistered by an out-of-control parent. No one was allowed to talk about what happened behind closed doors, and children had to just quietly wear the bruises and welts until they healed.

3

If Only We Could Fly

Judith and Vivian had discovered the game of "Mystery Dare" a few summers ago. They were lying in bed, the heavy cotton sheets sticking to their bodies and the oscillating electric fan blowing hot air around the room. It was too warm to sleep and they both were full of energy. They whispered in the dark, trying not to awaken their grandmother who shared the room.

"Scoot over some!" Viv complained. "You're all sweaty."

"Yeah, well you're sweaty too. That's probably why I'm sweaty, from being too close to you!"

"Well, everybody's sweaty, I guess. How can they even sleep?" The steady hum of snoring from the boys' room next to theirs was annoying when they were just twisting and turning, uncomfortable in their bed. The rest of the house was quiet and dark, the family content to dream the night away, but they wanted adventure. Nothing interesting ever happened at night, except for the sound of the scary antique clock that hung on the wall in Grandmother's room. When it announced the hour, its rusted spring wound itself tight and sounded like a warning of the entrance of Dracula.

"I wish we could fly," said Viv. "We could unhook the window screen, climb out onto the roof, and spread our wings."

"Where would you go if you could fly?"

"Oh, I don't know. I think I would like to just explore other people's houses, see where they keep their secret things."

"That would be fun. I would sneak in and change something in their house, so when they woke up things would look different and they wouldn't know why." They whispered like this in the dark, each trying to outdo the other with fantastic plots. The idea they settled on, and realized they could actually do, was pretty simple. They could unhook the window screen beside their bed, slip out onto the roof, and sit out there under the stars. They would still have to whisper because Grandmother was actually right there and might hear them.

It was considered Grandmother's room even though they slept in it and she had a little twin bed in the corner. Still it was her room, with their bed taking up most of it. Grandmother was a bear if they woke her at night. She got up very early every morning, slipped on her white uniform, and headed out to cook and clean for a white family across town. She needed her rest. If they woke her she would stand over their bed, shaking her fist at them and threatening to use it. She'd even call them names. She never used the "N-word" although they half expected her to, but she didn't mind calling them wenches and pissy-tailed gals.

"You see this fist?" she would say. "Feel of it!" and they would each have to take a turn feeling her fist, holding back giggles because they knew this was no real threat. Their dad would not allow her to really hit them with a fist. Any adult in the neighborhood had the freedom to give them a whuppin' with a switch from a nearby tree, and that was the limit—but if their dad ever knew they climbed out on the roof, they would be grounded for the entire summer, and it was that idea that made it more of an adventure.

And so they did it. The window squeaked as they raised it as high as it would go and they stopped, holding their breath as they waited for a response from Grandmother. She turned over on her side to face the opposite wall, and they proceeded with their plan. Quietly unhooking the window screen, they slithered out onto the roof. Viv went first because she was the smaller of the two and fit so easily through the window. But Jude quickly followed, and before they knew it, they had succeeded! They were outside the house, on the roof, under the stars. They were free!

The girls spent a few nights on the roof giggling and whispering before they both realized that the excitement had waned and they needed more of a challenge. This was the birth of "Mystery Dare." It was Jude's idea; she was the one who took things just a bit further. It would be a way to survive summer nights, she said, when the house was too quiet, the air was too hot and still, and they were wide awake.

"How about this?" Jude whispered. "If we jump down from this roof, we will only fall onto soft grass. It won't hurt us at all. We can have an adventure then climb up the posts on the front porch and back through the window. No one would ever know." Viv liked the idea. "Okay, but what adventure? What will we do out there?"

"Well, I dare you to come up with one," Jude said. So it was Viv who created the first dare: "I dare you to pick every flower in Mr. Pyle's garden." Mr. Pyle was a florist who lived next door; he provided flowers for the altars of the colored churches on Sundays and for all the colored funerals. His yard smelled of roses, carnations, and hyacinths and was beautiful even in moonlight.

Jude did it. They slipped down from the roof and Viv watched while she made her way across the yard, the moon lighting her way, and climbed Mr. Pyle's chain-link fence. She picked all the flowers she could carry. Then Jude placed the pile on the back step and both girls hurried to shinny up the post on the front porch, crawl along the roof to their bedroom window, and slip back inside. Once back in bed—with Grandmother quietly snoring, her back still turned to them—they eased out of bed then tiptoed down the stairs and through the dark downstairs rooms. The bathroom light was on and the door was closed, which could have meant that someone was up, but their mother always left it on to confuse any would-be burglars. Jude and Viv stood quietly beside the closed door, listening for any sound that would indicate someone was in there. Content that they were the only ones up, they hurried to the back door, unlocked it, and quietly sneaked the flowers in. The girls placed them in vases around the house and slipped back up to bed. They never admitted they knew how the flowers got there.

That was an easy dare, but over time the dares got harder and more dangerous. When it was Jude's turn, she gave Viv a scary one.

"Okay," she said. "Here's what you have to do. I dare you to go to Miss Whitmore's house at midnight and sit in the porch swing. You have to sit there for three minutes." Everyone knew the creaky old Whitmore house was haunted. Miss Whitmore had been dead for only a few months, but the house had been neglected for years. The paint had peeled away, shutters had come loose, and the house looked as old as Miss Whitmore herself. Her son, Mr. Whitmore, drank himself to death in that house a year before she died, and she had aged quickly after that.

They would see her each morning hunched over and still in her nightgown and robe as she picked up persimmons that had fallen from the tree in her yard, placing them in a crumpled paper sack on her porch. She would sit in the house, watching from the window to see which children found them. It was hard to be the ones who got there first because the Edwards girls lived next door. This solitary highlight of her day was not enough to keep her going, and finally she stopped. She died alone in that house, and there were rumors that the ghosts of the Whitmores sat in there in the dark with the cobwebs, the spiders, and old human bones. The house looked scary even in daylight, but at midnight, the girls were sure it would come alive.

"Are you going too?" Vivian's voice was already shaky, but she wasn't actually backing down.

"I'm going to sit on the curb and watch to see if you really do it." The moon lit the way, and the singing of crickets was the only sound they heard as the town slept. They walked barefoot in their pajamas the two blocks to Miss Whitmore's house, dew from the damp grass seeping between their toes. Jude sat across the street on the curb, her wet feet collecting gravel from the gutter, as she watched Viv make her way up onto the porch and finally sit in the swing.

The swing hung in front of the living room window. A lid of rusted, torn window screen covered it like an eye without a socket, silently watching the world outside. Vivian sat there counting the seconds, *One Mississippi, two Mississippi, three Mississippi* . . . until she was sure she had survived the three minutes, knowing that the ghosts of mother and son sat just on the other side of the window watching her. Her voice was shaky as relief and fear washed over her on the walk back home, and she talked about the smell of the place and how the swing creaked with every breath.

4

It's My Town

Every summer they took turns challenging each other to try things, and now this dare came to Jude: "I dare you to go to the Temple Theatre, get in and sit in a seat. Bring back proof." No colored person had ever set foot in the Temple Theatre. It was not allowed. The Rex Theatre was open to them, and that's where they went to watch the Saturday serials and Sunday matinees. There they would walk past the front of the theater, brightly lit with huge posters advertising the latest movies. They would pass the white people in line at the box office, hear their chatter and excitement, and see the fountain of popcorn in the lobby billowing out to be scooped up into red-and-white striped boxes. They would walk past all that excitement and enter through a side door, where they paid thirty-five cents and made their way up to the balcony reserved for colored people.

Every colored child in town had dreamed all their lives of going into the Temple, and it had become personal to Jude. There was something about being excluded that deeply disturbed her.

Whenever she stepped outside her own neighborhood, she was surrounded by signs that said "Whites only" or "Colored only." She had come to even resent those that said "Employees only." She didn't even want in—it was just the exclusion that bothered her. She just wanted to open the door, to step inside. She envied the white children she saw walk past her house, knowing they weren't aware of their freedom, their privilege to go wherever they wanted without restrictions.

On Saturday afternoons her mother took her, Viv, and their baby brother past the Temple on the bus to shop at the downtown stores. It was a Saturday tradition, a time to gather on street corners and catch up on each other's lives. The older boys went on their bikes. The rest of them dropped their dimes into the slot and marched to the back of the bus, pretending the white people sitting in the front weren't there. They pretended they didn't want to sit in the front, and that they didn't see the sign that said *WHITES START LOADING FROM FRONT. COLORED START LOADING FROM REAR.*

She loved the bus ride downtown but dreaded passing the Temple. The building loomed up huge and sacred like an ancient pyramid on the left side of the street, a white stucco monument to segregation with at least twenty steps leading up and into the building on two sides. The steps were flanked by enormous stone lions with odd-looking heads, protecting the magnificent treasures of gold and silver and diamonds that must be inside.

Because she wasn't allowed in, she created the interior in her mind. She knew it must be grand, something they were not considered good enough to see. The curtains at the windows would be made of thick, heavy red velvet with gold tassels and a long golden fringe. The floor was thickly carpeted with a fancy pattern like the one in the lobby of the Goldman Hotel where Daddy worked. There were crystal chandeliers all along the ceiling, which was painted with images of angels, huge white feathered wings protecting cuddly pink babies. The arms of the seats were made of engraved silver like the family's silver service used only on holidays. Seats were thick with velvet cushions. It had ushers, of course, who wore fancy red uniforms like that boy on TV who yelled out "CALL FOR PHILLIP MO-R-R-IS!" She imagined the moviegoers in tuxedos and ball gowns lounging around the theater and being served martinis with olives in thin crystal glasses. She had imagined this all her life, and now, on a Wednesday night in July 1953, she would see it for herself. She didn't know how she would get in; she'd just have to figure it out.

On the night of the dare, she waited in bed, tense with anticipation and fear, listening to her grandmother snore, until all she could hear was the humming of fans and the combined breaths of the family sucking the house into their dreams and softly turning it loose as they exhaled. As Viv watched, Jude raised the window, unlatched the screen, and slipped soundlessly to the soft grass. Viv came quietly out the window behind her. She dropped a bag of supplies for Jude to catch: a flashlight, a screwdriver, her shoes and socks and a peanut butter and jelly sandwich. Jude sat on the grass, putting on socks and shoes and trying to feel brave. She knew that her little sister was braver than she was, but she would never admit it to anyone, and hated to admit it to herself. She had to prove to herself that she could do this.

Already her breath was coming in short, quick puffs, and her heart pounded loud enough to wake her parents. The dampness of the grass penetrated her jeans and underwear and felt cool against her skin. She wanted to just sit there, enjoying the cool wet grass and watching the moon and stars move across the night sky. But she got up, placed the bag over her shoulder, then tiptoed past her parents' bedroom windows and out into the street.

All of their "mystery dares" had been done at night, so the walk along the quiet streets while the town slept was familiar to her. She gave her face to the soft coolness of the night air and thought about the people asleep in their houses. What were they dreaming? Maybe they were dreaming about a little colored girl taking matters into her own hands.

She pretended the town belonged to her. This was the town where Judge Parker had earned the title of the "Hanging Judge," had locked up Billy the Kid and Belle Starr. This was her town now. No one could tell her where to sit or drink, enter or exit. And no one would be hanged here. She imagined herself putting them all to sleep and rendering them powerless.

She heard her own footsteps against the pavement and watched her shadow grow, then loom gigantic ahead of her at each streetlight. Sometimes she hummed her favorite song to try to relax her shoulders and her breathing. *Last night I dreamed that I owned a candy store.* It was this song by an eight-year-old and recorded by Motown that convinced her she could become a famous singer. She was drawn up tight from head to toe, and her breath came in short bursts that could not penetrate her body below the chest. She had never broken into a building before.

An occasional passing car seemed to slow down and then move on. She forced her breathing to be slow and easy. She had a story ready that she had practiced several times to make it flow smoothly. *She was walking to her aunt's house to borrow a hot water bottle for her sick mother. No, she did not want a ride. Her mother did not allow her to get into the cars of strangers.* If they gave her any trouble she would run. But no one did.

5

A Sliver of Light

The Temple was a huge building that seemed as old as the town. It had been built in 1929 as a Masonic temple and was painted white to remind them every day which part of the population could enter. It had an auditorium with a stage, and white people had enjoyed movies there since before the girls were even born, but no colored person had ever set foot inside the building.

There were two entrances, each flanked by enormous statues of lions guarding the doors against colored intruders. The theater was eleven blocks away, and it would take awhile for Jude to even get there. She would never have considered this dare if it had come from someone else. Kids at school were always daring you to do some dumb thing. To them she would have said, "That's stupid. I don't take dares!" but she had to take this one seriously even though she knew the risks—or thought she did.

The building seemed much bigger at night, and the lions were more menacing. They looked as if they would come down from their perches and circle around her, baring their teeth, sizing her up. She didn't breathe at all as she walked past them and up to the front door as if it were the middle of the afternoon and she was all prepared to buy a ticket. Of course the doors were locked, but it was worth a try. They were double glass doors and she could see inside into the lobby, which had red carpeting. *She knew it would!* The walls were covered with framed posters of Audrey Hepburn in *Roman Holiday* and Marilyn Monroe in *How to Marry a Millionaire*. One wall held posters about *Nyoka, the Jungle Girl* and *Allan Rocky Lane*, the same Saturday serials she watched at the Rex. She tiptoed back down the steps as if the lions were sleeping and would eat her alive if she woke them up.

The side door, just like the front, was locked, and she was both relieved and disappointed. She noticed that drivers of the few cars that passed now were looking at her—probably wondering what she was doing, probably headed to a pay phone to call the police. The temperature had dropped some now and she could feel little bumps start to rise up on her arms—from cold or fear, she didn't know. She was about to lose the dare! She would have to go back empty-handed and face Viv, who would never let her live it down. Viv would go after her dares half-heartedly after this, and all the fun of it would slip away.

Jude wandered now around the back of the building, partly to avoid the eyes in the cars that passed and partly to kill time while she tried to come up with a really good story that would make her failed attempt still sound good. It was black dark back there away from the streetlights. She could hear the *swish, swish* of her tennis shoes on the wet grass and feel the cold on her feet as moisture seeped in through the cloth sides. She used the building itself as a guide through the dark and was so deep in thought she almost didn't see it. Without the blackness of the night she would have missed it altogether. There was a sliver of light—a long thin sliver. It started up higher than her head and went all the way to the ground.

The thought of an entrance didn't enter her head at first. She was just surprised and then curious. It was only as she moved closer to it that she realized that a door was open—a small door actually, although it was taller than she was. She had found a back entrance, maybe a place where the theater staff came and went. Someone had left it open, had left a light on. Jude's heart leapt in excitement as she rushed toward it, then stopped stock still. *Why would someone leave this open? Was this a trap? Had someone who saw me snooping around out front called the police, who are waiting inside with handcuffs and leg irons? Will they carry me off to some kind of prison camp like the one in* Stalag 17 *with William Holden, my parents never knowing what happened to me? They would think I just disappeared into the night!*

She looked around in the darkness and could find no evidence that there was anyone there. She listened and it took her awhile to filter out the pounding in her ears and the constant rush of air coming from her own breathing. Then the only thing she could hear was the sound of crickets and the crunch of tires on asphalt as a car whizzed past. *Well, I have to go in,* she thought. *Or how can I explain that I just walked away from the easiest entrance ever?* She held her breath, pushed the door open wider, and stepped through.

She found herself in a small room, with faded green walls stacked high with cardboard boxes. An old office chair with cotton poking through a hole in the plastic upholstery sat in front of a green metal desk. A crumpled, half-empty pack of Lucky Strikes lay beside an ashtray full of butts, and an open bottle of Old Crow stood beside a dingy smudged glass. The place smelled musty even with the door open, and before she could think it through, she sneezed. She froze and waited for footsteps, a voice, a door to slam—something. Nothing happened.

This was some kind of a storage room, and somebody had left it unlocked. She breathed a sigh of relief and took a tentative step toward a black metal door on the far wall. She opened it and slipped quietly through. Jude was eager to get this done, find some sort of proof and get out. This had been too easy, and that worried her. Something bad was bound to happen, and her only hope was to do this quickly and escape. She closed the heavy metal door behind her. If the drunk returned she didn't want to leave any evidence that anyone was here. Darkness swallowed her up. It was as if she had just walked into a tomb, a mausoleum, and all the spirits of the dead were awakened by her entrance. Or maybe it was the spirits of old movie heroes and heroines lingering in the halls, unable to tear themselves away from the memory of applause. But Jude knew she was not alone.

She felt her way down a hallway that slanted toward a swinging door. The theater had to be on the other side. She heard the door squeak as she pushed it open and stood there, making history. There should be cameras, lights, reporters, she thought. *The first colored person in history to stand inside the auditorium of the Temple Theatre!* If she were caught now, there would be, and although she would probably get life on a chain gang, the headlines would be worth it: COLORED GIRL BREAKS INTO CITY'S FINEST THEATRE. CAUGHT RED-HANDED. She knew Viv would find a joke in that somewhere. She almost wished it would happen. *I would go down in history with all the other firsts: Jackie Robinson, Mary McLeod Bethune, George Washington Carver—and me, Judith Johnson.*

The familiar sight of stairs leading up to the balcony brought her back to the moment, and through habit she headed toward them. She was halfway up when she realized she could have sat downstairs, but going back now would waste precious time, and she moved on, found the landing, felt her way to the nearest seat, and sank into it amazed that it was not cushioned, velvet, luxurious. As she sat there wondering what to do, how to find a souvenir, she realized she was cold. She had sneaked out of the house wearing only a T-shirt and jeans. *At least I didn't wear a dress*, she thought. She could feel her heart pounding through her clothes, and she thought she could probably see it pumping in and out except it was too dark. *Maybe I should get out of here*, she thought. But she'd come this far. It just didn't make sense to leave now, not without something to show for it.

The theater had been closed since eleven, and now it was empty. The seat she'd found felt foreign to her, too big. She knew the other seats were empty too, but she could feel the ghosts of the people who had sat in those seats just a few hours ago. The voices she was hearing in her own head seemed to be theirs telling her to get out: *You shouldn't be here. You're just a kid—and you're a girl—and you're colored—you don't belong here.*

But she would stay, and she would finish her job. It was only then that her eyes adjusted to the darkness, and she allowed herself the luxury of fully noticing the place. She felt the bottoms of her shoes against the floor. It's *not* carpeted. She lifted them and discovered it was also sticky. She would have expected that in the balcony of the Rex. No one ever cleaned that place with its sticky mixture and strange aroma of urine, vomit, and cola. *But who had to sit in the balcony of the Temple? Who spilled drinks up here, and who forgot to mop it up?* Things were not making sense.

Again she felt the presence of someone with her there. Was this her vivid imagination, or was she truly not alone? She forced herself to take a couple of deep breaths and heard only silence. So here was the hard part: what could she take? What would prove that she was really there and didn't just make up a great story to tell Viv? She had a flashlight and a screwdriver in her bag, but she didn't know if she could risk taking them out and shining a light around the place. *What about the drunk? Where is he?* It must have been at least 2 a.m., but Jude didn't have a watch. *Everybody but me is surely in bed,* she thought.

Jude waited for another sound and heard something like water dripping. There was the familiar clunk a hot water heater sometimes makes in the middle of the night, and there was definitely the ticking of a clock. She took the flashlight from her pocket and pushed the off-on switch forward. The beam of light shooting out like a sword before her illuminated a balcony just like the one at the Rex. *Where is the velvet, the engraved silver, the finery? What were they protecting in here?* Jude's heart sank. This was no victory. There was nothing here but a stinking theater balcony, one with cola spilled on the floor and soggy popcorn—probably smelly bathrooms too.

6

So You're a Girl!

She moved the light from seat to seat, across the ceiling and floor, toward the balcony ledge and over to the stairs. The light guided her across the aisles, across wooden plank floors, and across a pair of *brown work boots*. Jude was so preoccupied with her disappointment it took a moment for her to register that there were feet in those boots! The world stopped; nothing worked. She knew she hadn't died, but she could not move forward past this moment. The flashlight trembled in her hand and she could hardly keep it steady. Holding it with both hands, she moved it up the denim pants above the boot tops, the blue denim work shirt, and onto the round red face of a man with wispy brown hair around the edges of a bald head. *A white man,* his eyes blue marbles floating in a pink sea. They squinted at the light, and a short, fat hand moved to cover them.

"I'm sorry!" Jude almost screamed. "I—I don't know how I got in here. This is a mistake! Just let me get past you and I'll get out of here!" The words came bubbling out of her mouth, not powered by thought. "You'll never see me again. I promise. I was never here!" Even while she was babbling, she was trying to think of something she could snatch on the way out as proof that she was there. The man flipped a switch, and the place lit up.

"Calm down, son." His voice was loud and rough, but not really threatening. *Maybe he doesn't belong in here either.*

"You break in here too? You a hobo or something?" Jude asked.

"What I got to be answering your questions for? Seem to me you supposed to be answering some of mine."

She checked him over more carefully this time. There was no weapon that she could see. But he didn't seem friendly either. He could be here because he's in trouble, and he could cause trouble for her. The man sat down on the step now and slipped the half-pint of Old Crow from his hip pocket. Removing the cap, he lifted the bottle to his lips and took a deep draw from it, all in one motion. He replaced the cap and set the bottle carefully on the step beside him. Jude was quiet, waiting for his next move and looking around for another way out. She considered the leap over the balcony but quickly decided against it.

"Mister, I ain't looking for trouble. I don't need to know nothing about you. I just need to go home, that's all."

"No need to rush off, boy. Since we both here, we might's well get acquainted." A pause, then, "Frank." He stretched out his hand to her. She didn't take it.

"Pleased to meet you. Unlike you, I didn't break in here. I works here. Been working here nights for nigh onto fifteen years. Seen two, three colored boys a year sneak into this place. But you, you look like you scared half to death."

Jude kept her mouth shut, thinking about what he just said and not wanting to believe it. *Other kids? I'm not the first?*

"You thought you was the first little colored boy to come wandering in here, trying to see for yourself what's so special about this place, didn't you?"

"No, sir." Her voice was shaky as she answered, but she was thinking *I'm the first girl.* He looked at her more closely now as if he could hear her thoughts.

"Jesus H. Christ! You's a girl, ain't ya? Never had a girl sneak in here befo'!" He stumbled up from the step, rubbing his bald head and then the two-day stubble on his chin. Jude backed away. Every story her parents had ever told her about who to watch out for was looming up in front of her eyes. He fit the picture perfectly: *a man—a white man—a drunk white man. Probably a molester.* Now what? Her hands were too sweaty to hold onto the flashlight and she didn't need it anyway, so she let it slip to the floor beside her. The thud as it dropped caught her off guard, startling her to the point of screaming, her nerves already so tight she could hardly breathe. She hadn't expected it to be so loud, to echo like that in the empty building. But she swallowed the scream, almost choked on it while she willed her body to calm itself. She stood there unable to move, unable to think. She had turned to stone and was in the world of the great lion statues, frozen in concrete, in a moment that would last forever. She even wished for it, she and the lions safe in a world where nothing moves, nothing happens.

But her mind was not still. It was whirling with thought, whizzing through her mental files looking for anything under the heading of "Emergency Procedures."

"Yes sir, I'm a girl." She smiled, pretending to be friendly. *Maybe before he makes his move to grab me, tie me up, molest and kill me, then throw my body in the woods somewhere, I can run past him and out of here.* She still had the screwdriver in her bag. That might come in handy.

"I been in here lots of times," she lied. "This ain't my first time doin' this. You think I'm a sissy or something? You don't know how tough girls can be. I've done lots of things, and I been in here so many times I know my way all around this place." Despite an urge to run, here she was talking, but talking way too fast. He just looked at her then slowly shook his head.

"Naw, you ain't never been in here before." He laughed in a quiet way that sounded more like a clearing of his throat, and he looked her over again. "I seen how you looked all 'round the place. You don't know nothing 'bout me, neither. I ain't gone hurt you. Got no need to. I know you scared, girl. I don't blame you. I'd be scared too."

Jude was watching his every move now. What was he doing? Trying to trick her, so he could catch her off guard and grab her? His eyes seemed to shine as he checked her out, and he was real relaxed too. That was probably the booze. He leaned comfortably against the wall behind him, his arms folded across his chest, a slight smile tempting the corners of his mouth upward.

"Tell you what," he said. "You stay right there, and I'll go get you a grape Nehi and give you a real tour." He winked at her as he picked up his whiskey bottle and returned it to his hip pocket. He was standing just a few feet away, but she couldn't judge the degree of danger she might be in. The circumstances alone should be enough of a clue, but this old man was a little hard to figure out. He headed off down the steps toward the storage room door. She could run right now. She could make a beeline out of this place. This was her chance and maybe her only chance, but she stood right there. Maybe it was the wink, or the way he knew she was lying, or maybe she just couldn't pass up the tour. Something about him seemed friendly, so against everything her parents had ever taught her to do, she waited.

Jude hadn't waited long when he returned with a grape soda in one hand and a box of popcorn in the other. He had a big smile on his face and held them out for her to take. She was surprised at her eagerness to get them, not realizing until now that she was hungry and had forgotten all about the sandwich in her bag.

7

Everybody's Got Secrets

"Come on," he said and headed back down the steps. She followed him as he moved excitedly around the place, ending at the little room way above the balcony with the projector and lots of dusty rolls of film lying in stacks in the corners. She had had a little trouble keeping up, but Frank didn't seem to notice as he went on and on about the theater. He talked about all the movies he'd seen and all the scripts he knew by heart.

"I know them characters better than I ever knowed any real folks," he said, proudly.

"If I could be friends with a movie star, I would choose Gene Autry," Jude told him. "I've been to see every Gene Autry movie there is." She was relaxing now too. Frank looked at her and smiled. She thought he was going to launch into some story about Gene Autry, but he moved on to how the theater looked when it was shiny and new. Jude wasn't at all impressed with this place. All her dreams of grandeur had been wiped away with the flick of a light switch. No velvet, no angels painted on the ceiling, no nothing.

Frank talked constantly about the theater, himself, his life, folks he knew. It sounded to Jude like he didn't get to talk to people much. She was guessing that when he got the chance he had to grab it and say everything at once.

"Ain't much to see, is it?" Frank paused to face her. She had nothing to say—the facts were too obvious: faded torn curtains, dirty old wood floors, and just regular old seats. This place was a dump. She wondered about the logic of not letting colored folks come into this dump of a theater. It looked like they could use some more paying customers.

"You done a pretty scary thing coming in here in the middle of the night. I mean this must be the scariest thing a little girl like you could think of to do. You couldn't be more'n ten, eleven years old." Jude couldn't believe he had her mixed up with a ten-year-old. She was going to be a teenager next year.

"I'm twelve!" she said, indignant.

"I guess twelve-year-olds is pretty brave then, huh? Coming in here like that."

"I guess I am," Jude answered like it might be a fact, although she wasn't so sure.

"Lots of folks is brave, I guess, but I ain't one of them." He was off again, talking about himself. Jude had finished her popcorn but was too polite to ask for more.

They were sitting on rolls of film in the dusty projection room. "I ain't all that brave, either," she said. Being in this theater was the bravest thing she had ever done in her life, but she knew there were harder things to do, things she couldn't do at all. She told him about how much her mother wanted her to be ladylike and to make speeches and recite poetry at church. She just couldn't do it. She could memorize anything, and she could recite it back easily to Viv, but standing up on a stage with a crowd of people looking at her—it was too hard. She felt too self-conscious in ruffles and lace, patent leather shoes, her hair all done up in ribbons. That was the one thing her mamma wanted from her, and it was just too hard.

Frank took another swig from his bottle and she sipped her grape Nehi, trying to savor it. It was actually Jude's favorite pop in the whole world, next to Grapette, so she was working hard to make it last.

"Since you talking to me now," he said, "how about tell me how a little colored girl ended up here in the middle of the night swapping stories with an old bum like me? You wasn't too scared to come in here, so tell me how come."

"I can't tell you that," she said. "It's a secret between me and my sister, and I don't even know you. I can't tell you that."

"Everybody's got secrets," Frank said. "How 'bout I tell you one of mine, and then maybe you can trust me with yours?" Frank fumbled for the Lucky Strikes in his shirt pocket, and then for a matchbook. It seemed like a ritual the way he shook out the filter-less cigarette, tapped down the loose tobacco, and struck the match on his fingernail then took a long draw. Loose tobacco stuck to his bottom lip. Jude thought he had gone away inside his head, looking for a suitable secret to share with her, and couldn't find one.

8

Sharing Secrets

PP

A in't much of a secret really," he said. "I should'a done
something and I didn't is all." Frank was standing
up now, for some reason, and Jude thought he was
through talking. She half expected him to say he'd better be
getting on with his work and she should leave now and go
on home. But he just walked around in a circle as if he'd lost
something. He sat back down and started to talk again.

"I grew up right here, just like you, and my folks hated folks
like you," he said softly. Jude knew she was in trouble now. She
knew she should have left a long time ago and not gotten taken
in by an old drunk's stories.

"Folks I grew up with thought you little nig'ra babies was born
with a tail." Jude was ready to go now, didn't want to hear any
more. She had gotten up to leave when he continued.

"I made a slingshot when I was a boy 'bout ten. Didn't call it
no slingshot, though. Called it a 'nigger shooter.'" *Why is he
telling me this? I'm scared enough, just being here. What is he*

doing? "I carried it with me everywhere I went, and any time I saw one of y'all, I shot him with it. I thought I was a pretty brave boy." Again he stopped, and Jude inched toward the door.

"When I turned twenty-one my friends gave a big party for me. They came over early and decorated our living room with crepe paper and balloons. Some of 'em brought beer and pop and put it on ice in a big wash tub in the kitchen. It wasn't no surprise party. I knowed they was going to do it 'cause everybody had been saving up for about a month, even me. It was a good party though, and we drunk all the booze we had. In fact, it was the only party I ever had in my life and the most fun I ever had too, until things began to slow down around midnight." Frank was into his story now, and so was Jude. She had sat back down and waited to hear what happened next.

"Folks was 'bout drunk by then. I was pretty near ready to turn in myself, knowing I'd had way more liquor under my belt than I ought to have when ol' Carl said, 'Let's go have some fun.'" Frank stopped, took a long drag from his Lucky Strike, and looked at her.

"Maybe I shouldn't be telling you this," he said. "I can stop here if you want me to."

"You have to finish it now," she said. She was scared to hear the rest of Frank's story but felt like she had to know how it ended. Frank dropped his cigarette butt on the floor, stepped on it and then went through the whole ritual again of tapping in the loose tobacco, striking the match, and lighting up. Jude thought he was stalling. Maybe he wasn't as worried about her hearing the story as he was about his ability to tell it.

"Everybody got all excited and before I knew anything, we had piled into the back of Carl's pickup and was headed out to find some fun. I had a bad feeling about this, but I didn't want to let my buddies down neither."

"What happened?" Jude asked.

"We tricked a colored boy into accepting a ride. He was walking home from the swing shift over at Dixie Cup. He looked like he was tired. He wore a pair of dirty coveralls and smelled of sweat. I never knowed what work he done. He grinned when we offered him a lift and jumped right onto the truck bed with me and Freeman. He thanked us right off for the ride, telling us about his folks waiting for him at home. He seemed kinda slow. It wasn't until we headed towards the woods that his expression changed and he stopped talking right in the middle of a sentence. I remember he started saying 'Naw, naw' over and over again."

Jude was through listening to this story. She already knew how this was going to end, and she got up to leave.

"I'm gonna go now, Frank. I'm not brave." She could feel her stomach tightening around all the popcorn and grape soda she'd consumed. "I—I can't hear this."

"You feeling just like I did then. You feeling like you gonna throw up. And that's what I done. I leaned over the side of the truck and I throwed up." Frank went on as if he didn't hear Jude's protests. She was standing up now, heading toward the exit, and yet he was still talking and Jude found herself still listening.

"Maybe I just had too much to drink. Maybe it was everything just moving too fast before I had a chance to think it through. I was the one that got him into the truck. I give him a big smile and asked him if he wanted a ride. I give him my hand and boosted him up beside me. He sat down in the back of the pickup and that was when it hit me. I had never in my life touched one of 'em before. I never had really talked to one of 'em, or looked one of 'em in the eye. He seemed like a pretty nice fella too."

The story was pouring out of Frank now—there was no stopping him.

"I lost my nerve. I tried to stop it. I even begged Carl and Freeman and the others not to do it, to just let him go, but they ignored me. I could only stand and watch while they did it. They was all drunk, you know. They built a fire. I didn't even know the boy's name. He was curled up in a ball. He moaned and cried while Freeman and the others tied his hands and feet. I watched until it all became a blur to me, all the laughing and liquor, the kicking and whooping and scurrying around. It just was swirling around in my head and I was doing nothing, just sitting on the pickup bed being as scared as the boy on the ground."

Jude tried to put herself in Frank's place, tried to feel what he must have felt, but she found herself looking up at Frank from the ground, curled up in a ball, unable to move with her feet bound and her hands bound. She found herself thinking about her family and how they might be wondering where she was, how they would never know what happened if she didn't show back up at home. She could see delirious white men in overalls, barefoot with no shirts, tossing a rope over the limb of a tree, stopping to pass a bottle around and then heading toward her.

She felt herself give in and begin to just endure rather than to fight. She watched the shadows cast by the bonfire against the truck and surrounding woods. She saw them pause to have a cigarette and congratulate each other on becoming men, and she took a break too. She just died early, took an early exit so as not to join them in the deed.

"I didn't stop them," Frank said. Tears had filled his eyes and had begun to run down his flushed cheeks. He had no idea where Jude was, didn't know he had taken her straight to death and made her look it in the eye, forced her to face a fear she never knew was there. In that moment the boredom of her neighborhood became purposeful.

"Every moment I thought I would stop them," he said, "but I couldn't do it. When they set his clothes on fire . . ." He stood up and walked to the other side of the room, paced for a while and sat back down again. He stared at his work boots. "That's when my bladder went," he said.

Jude didn't look at Frank, knowing it would embarrass him. They both looked at the floor.

"I lost my friends that night. I couldn't live with what I seen. The next morning I got up early, went straight into town and turned myself in. I turned them in, too. Nothing happened to them. Everything happened to me. I lost my job. My folks disowned me as a coward, and my best friend became Mr. Old Crow, here." Frank patted his hip pocket as if he genuinely believed that bottle loved him.

"I didn't find work for a long time, but this job opened up and it was one where no one had to be around me. I took it. I know the stories of just about every movie around, and sometimes I feel closer to them characters on the screen than I ever have to anyone in real life."

9

A New Challenge

They sat silently looking at each other. Frank found a dingy handkerchief in a pocket and wiped his eyes and blew his nose. Jude watched him, feeling faint and not sure how to move past this moment. She wiped her own eyes on her T-shirt and discovered she was dripping with sweat. The fear of being caught in this theater had taken on new meaning for her. The world she thought she knew had expanded in a way she couldn't fully process. The pounding of her heart was no longer about the dare; it was about how to live in the world—who she was, and what it meant in this town. She thought about those movie characters Frank called his friends. Movie characters have happy endings most of the time. People get rewarded for good deeds and don't get away with murder. She looked at the stacks of film cases, Frank's friends, and felt grateful for the safety of her living, breathing neighborhood, people that she knew loved and protected her.

"I never told that story from start to finish to no one before. I guess I was too ashamed of myself. I didn't care if people didn't want to be 'round me, 'cause I didn't want to be 'round myself, and I didn't want folks to see that I was all soft inside. I couldn't be around men no more because I knowed I wasn't like them. My heart was different. I still see that fella sometimes in my dreams, and I'm always trying to say I'm sorry."

Jude sat for a moment in silence, her voice struggling to find its way out of her throat, timid and hoarse, thirsty for air. "Well, you said it to me," she whispered. Frank looked like he had been miles away.

"Yeah, I guess I did," he said. "If there's something you think is right to do, you got to do it, you know? Even if it don't work out in the end." Jude nodded, and Frank stood up as if they had ended the night and it was time to wrap things up. Jude stood up too, not sure her legs would hold her. She realized that it might be daylight outside, and she was in trouble if people at home were awake before she got back. She wasn't worried anymore about what could happen to her there, just what would happen if she didn't get back home in time. She followed Frank out of the projection room and down the steps toward the exit, then stopped, taking one last look at the stage. Frank looked at her.

"I dare you," he said. He looked like a kid himself egging her on. He had no idea what those words meant to Jude, but they were the right ones.

"There aren't any spotlights," she said.

"I got all kinds of lights in here," and he was already on his way back up the stairs. Jude hesitated then headed toward the stage, found the steps to the right side of it and moved toward the curtain that hid the screen. She thought about Tony Harper, the eight-year-old colored girl who made a Top Ten 45 record. On one side was "Dolly's Lullaby," and on the other was "Candy Store Blues." The lights came up and blinded her. She couldn't see beyond the circle of light surrounding her, but she imagined a full theater cheering and clapping.

"Last night I dreamed that I owned a candy store . . ." She belted it out. She knew every word of that song, had sung it on the imaginary stage in her bedroom a million times. The applause at the end came from only one set of hands and lungs, but she loved it. Jude ran off the stage and down the steps, knowing she was just not scared anymore—not of Frank, not of anything.

At the narrow back door she remembered the proof for her sister and turned back. She saw Frank approaching behind her and before she could ask, he stopped her.

"Wait," he said and headed toward the old metal desk. He opened a drawer, shuffled through clutter, and emerged with a photograph—not of himself but of Gene Autry. It was autographed.

"I been keeping this way too long," he said. "No reason you shouldn't have it now."

"I can't take this," Jude said. It would be the perfect proof, but she knew it was pretty important to Frank too. It was wrinkled and smudged as if he'd held it for long hours. She walked back to the desk, and finding an old ballpoint pen, she turned the picture over and leaned over the desk. She carefully printed "Thanks, Frank." She signed her own autograph, Judith Ann Johnson, and handed him back the picture. Frank took it again and read it, then with a big grin, he returned it to the drawer. He shook his head and opened the door for Jude.

Jude was guided by the light from the doorway until she reached the streetlamps and took off in a trot. The darkness had faded to gray, and she would need to be in her bed by the time her grandmother got up, yawning and stretching as if this had all been a dream. She thought about the picture of Gene Autry, and sort of wished she had kept it, but it felt right that she didn't. She knew she was not returning empty-handed and she wondered if Viv would see the proof in her, that she had come back changed.

She went through their routine of climbing the posts on the front porch, almost ran toward the window that was still open waiting for her return. She wiggled through it and back under the covers beside her sister. Too tired to talk, she hugged Viv, and Viv hugged her back. She knew they would talk later, but now she closed her eyes and let Frank and his story and her own story and the story of her town adjust themselves in her tired mind and her tired body. Sleep was what she needed to sort it out, but she knew that tomorrow and the next day and the day after that she would be ready for whatever came.

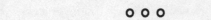

Acknowledgments

So many thanks to the members of my writing group who traveled this road with me.

To Linda Leavell, Nancy Hartney, Peggy Konert, Ann Teague, Rebecca Harrison, and Dewayne Keirn, gifted writers who cheered me on, encouraged me, and loved me through the process.

To Kent Landrum, who passed on before I could thoroughly thank him for being my champion but who always recognized my uniqueness and encouraged me to trust my voice.

To my family, who read my drafts, and shaped my words, my thoughts, and my heart as my characters developed through parts of their lives and hearts.

To Fort Smith, a whole community who cradled me from the first time I sat down to write a book at age nine, and gently gave me the experiences that were crucial to having a story to tell.

And finally, to Casie Dodd and her team, who were patient and encouraging as we made this book a reality.

DOROTHY DODSON MARCY is a licensed professional counselor and writer of short stories. She holds a bachelor's degree in English and French from Northwestern State University and a master's in counselor education from the University of Arkansas. Born in Fort Smith, Arkansas, she now lives in Fayetteville. She has been a contributor to KUAF National Public Radio's *Ozarks at Large* and the magazine *Arkansas Life*.

Belle Point Press is a literary small press
along the Arkansas-Oklahoma border.
Our mission is simple: Stick around and read.
Learn more at bellepointpress.com.